MICHAEL JOSEPH LTD

Published by the Penguin Group
27 Wrights Lane, London W8 5TZ, England
Viking Penguin Inc., 40 West 23rd Street, New York, New York 10010, USA
Penguin Books Australia Ltd, Ringwood, Victoria, Australia
Penguin Books Canada Ltd, 2801 John Street, Markham, Ontario, Canada L3R 1B4
Penguin Books (NZ) Ltd, 182–190 Wairau Road, Auckland 10, New Zealand

Penguin Books Ltd, Registered Offices: Harmondsworth, Middlesex, England

First published 1989

Typeset in Linotron Garamond Light ITC
by Goodfellow & Egan, Cambridge

Colour reproduction by Anglia Graphics, Bedford
Printed and bound in Italy by L.E.G.O.

A CIP catalogue record for this book is available from the British Library
ISBN 0 7181 3333 1
Library of Congress catalog number 89-84116

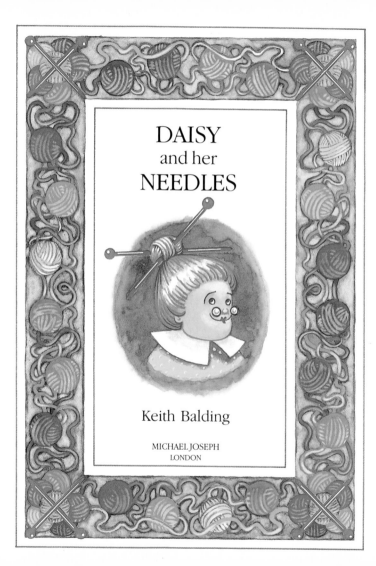

DAISY
and her
NEEDLES

Keith Balding

MICHAEL JOSEPH
LONDON

When Daisy got out her needles
The world began to change

She knitted
a fire

She knitted
her tea

She knitted
her husband

And she knitted
me

When Daisy got out her needles
The world became quite woolly

She knitted
some books

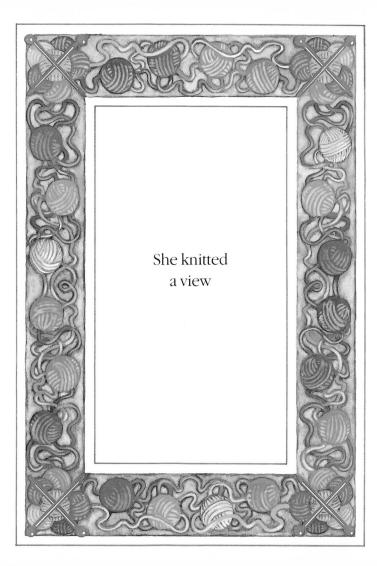

She knitted
a view

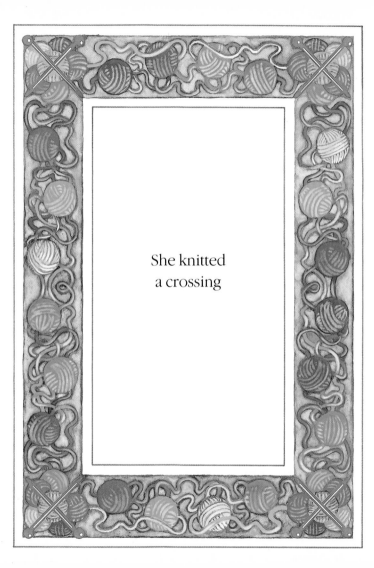

She knitted
a crossing

And she knitted
a ewe

As Daisy worked hard at her
needles
The world began to soften

She knitted
a garden

She knitted
a gnome

She knitted
a prize

And she knitted
a home

She knitted a scene
From an avant-garde
ballet

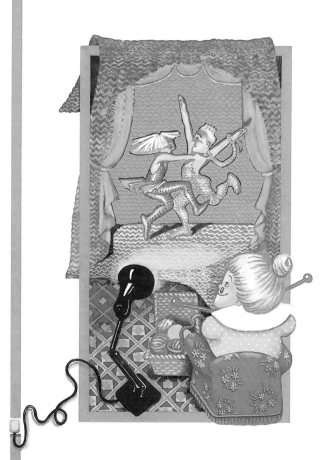

She knitted a clock
In the shape of a chalet

She knitted a plate
With a birthday cake on it

She knitted a cat
With a bonnet upon it

She knitted a tree
With the apples all rosy

And just for a change
Another tea cosy

Daisy has knitted
And this book is full
So she's busily knitting
Some new balls of wool

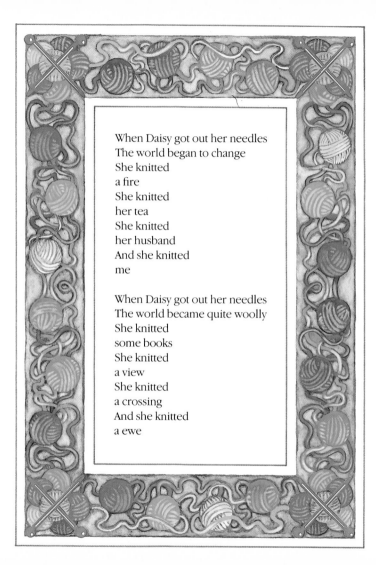

When Daisy got out her needles
The world began to change
She knitted
a fire
She knitted
her tea
She knitted
her husband
And she knitted
me

When Daisy got out her needles
The world became quite woolly
She knitted
some books
She knitted
a view
She knitted
a crossing
And she knitted
a ewe

As Daisy worked hard at her needles
The world began to soften
She knitted
a garden
She knitted
a gnome
She knitted
a prize
And she knitted
a home

She knitted a scene
From an avant-garde ballet
She knitted a clock
In the shape of a chalet
She knitted a plate
With a birthday cake on it
She knitted a cat
With a bonnet upon it
She knitted a tree
With the apples all rosy
And just for a change
Another tea cosy

Daisy has knitted
And this book is full
So she's busily knitting
Some new balls of wool